For Carol Anthony

Clarion Books
Ticknor & Fields, a Houghton Mifflin Company
Text and illustrations copyright © 1988 by Dick Gackenbach

Library of Congress Cataloging-in-Publication Data
Gackenbach, Dick.
Harvey, the foolish pig.

Summary: A poor pig goes on a journey to ask
the Great King for wealth but fails to recognize
the riches offered to him along the way.
[1. Wealth—Fiction.   2. Pigs—Fiction]   I. Title.
PZ7.G117 Harr   1988 [E]   87-15691
ISBN 0-89919-540-7

Y 10 9 8 7 6 5 4 3 2 1

HARVEY,
the Foolish Pig

Retold and Illustrated by DICK GACKENBACH

CLARION BOOKS/TICKNOR & FIELDS/NEW YORK

Once there was a pig named Harvey. Harvey was an ordinary pig except that he was poorer than most. His trousers were covered in patches and he had no shoes.

Harvey hated being poor and wanted to be rich. So one day he decided to go in search of the wise and great King of Animals.

"I will ask the King a question," Harvey told himself. "I will ask him how I, Harvey Pig, can become rich."

That very day Harvey set off to find the King.

Soon after Harvey began his journey, he met a hungry wolf. "Where are you going?" the wolf asked the pig.

"To find the wise King of Animals," replied Harvey. "I have a question to ask him!"

"Well," said the wolf, "when you find him, ask him a question for me, too. Tell the King you met a hungry wolf who doesn't have a thing to eat. Ask him if he knows where I can find a good meal."

Harvey nodded. "I will," he promised. And then he went on his way.

A little farther along, Harvey met a pretty pig named Louella.

"Sit and stay a while," Louella invited Harvey.

"I'm in a hurry," he answered. "I must find the wise King of Animals. I have a question to ask him."

"Go then," said Louella, "but when you find the King ask him a question for me as well. Tell him I am very pretty and very rich, but I am very unhappy. Ask him what will make me happy."

Harvey promised Louella he would ask the King, and then he continued his journey.

Next Harvey met a thirsty tree. Even though it was summer, the tree's leaves were parched and brown.

"Where are you going in such a rush?" the tree asked the pig.

"To find the wise King of Animals," said Harvey. "I have a question to ask him."

"Ah," said the tree. "And when you find him will you ask a question for a poor tree, too?"

"All right," said Harvey. He hoped he could keep all the questions straight.

"Then tell the King you met a tree that lives by the side of a river, yet is always dry and thirsty. Ask him if my leaves will ever turn green again."

Harvey gave the tree his promise and then rushed on, for he was anxious to find the King.

At last, after passing over meadows bright with sunshine and forests deep in shadows, Harvey found the wise King.

The little pig knelt before His Majesty and waited for him to speak.

"Greetings, Pig!" said the Protector of All Creatures. "The birds have told me of your journey. Why do you seek me out?"

"Well," said Harvey, "the world is full of riches while I have patches on my trousers and can afford no shoes."

"That is so," remarked the King.

"Then, sir," pleaded Harvey, "may I not have some riches, too?"

"I will give you the Gift of Good Luck," replied the King. "If you deserve them, you may have all the riches you will ever need. But," he warned, "you must find them first."

"Where will I look for them?" asked Harvey.

"Keep your eyes and ears open, and use your head," said the King. "They will show you the way. Now be off with you."

Before Harvey departed to find his riches, he remembered his promise and asked the King the questions for the hungry wolf, the beautiful Louella, and the dry tree.

The King listened patiently while scratching his mane. Then he gave Harvey three wise answers to take back with him.

Harvey thanked the King and hurried off to search for his riches.

The thirsty tree was happy to see the pig return.

"What answer did the King send me?" the tree asked Harvey.

"He told me to tell you there is a pot of gold buried beneath your roots," explained Harvey. "Until it is removed, no water will ever reach your leaves and you will not bear fruit again."

The tree's limbs began to shake.

"What are you waiting for?" he shouted. "Remove the gold, you foolish pig."

"No, no," said Harvey. "I have no time. I must go and find my riches."

And off he ran.

Louella Pig was eagerly awaiting Harvey's return, too.

"Does the King have an answer for me?" she asked.

"Yes," replied Harvey. "He told me to tell you that you are unhappy because you are lonely. He said you should find someone to share your life with you. Only then will you be happy."

"Marry me then," Louella pleaded, "and we will both be happy."

"I'm sorry, but I can't right now," said Harvey as he ran away. "I must find my riches!"

"Oh, you foolish pig," said Louella sadly.

Farther down the road, Harvey met the hungry wolf again.

"What does the King have to say to me?" asked the wolf. "Did he send me a good meal?"

"Oh, so much has happened," said Harvey, sitting down to catch his breath. "On my way to see the King, I met Louella Pig who was so unhappy despite her wealth and beauty. Then I met a thirsty tree who wanted to know how to get some water.

"Well," continued Harvey, "the King told me to tell the tree to remove a pot of gold from beneath its roots, and he told me to tell Louella to get herself a husband. Then and only then would Louella be happy and the tree would get water. WHEW!"

"And did you tell them?" asked the wolf.

"I did indeed!" replied Harvey. "And Louella wanted me to marry her, and the tree wanted me to remove the gold."

"What did you do?" asked the wolf.

"I had to refuse, of course," said Harvey. "The King gave me the Gift of Good Luck and I am in a hurry to find my riches."

"Well, before you go," said the wolf, "what did the King have to say to me?"

"Oh yes," said Harvey. "I almost forgot. The King told me to tell you that you may meet a foolish pig with patches on his trousers and no shoes who doesn't know his good luck when he sees it."

"Then what?" asked the wolf eagerly. "Then what does the King say I should do?"

"Eat him!" said Harvey.

THE END